WOW!

SAID THE OWL

For Wanda, with love

With thanks to Celia Catchpole,
and all at Macmillan Children's Books,
especially Emily Ford and Kayt Manson.

First published 2009 by Macmillan Children's Books
a division of Macmillan Publishers Limited
20 New Wharf Road, London N1 9RR
Basingstoke and Oxford
Associated companies throughout the world
www.panmacmillan.com

ISBN: 978-1-4472-5914-5

Text and illustrations copyright © Tim Hopgood 2009
Moral rights asserted.

10 9 8 7 6 5 4 3 2 1

A CIP catalogue record for this book is available
from the British Library.

Printed in China

WOW!
SAID THE OWL

tim hopgood

MACMILLAN CHILDREN'S BOOKS

At night, when we are feeling tired and ready for bed, owls are just waking up.

Owls live in a night-time world.

They have eyes that can see in the dark.

But this little owl was a curious owl.

Instead of staying awake all night, as little owls are supposed to do, she took a long nap and woke up just before dawn.

"WOW!" said the owl.

She couldn't believe her eyes!
The sky was a warm and wonderful **pink**.

"WOW!" said the owl,
as the **yellow** sun shone
through the morning mist.

"WOW!" said the owl,
as **white** fluffy clouds floated
across the bright **blue** sky.

"WOW!" said the owl,
when she saw that the leaves
on her tree were **green**.

"WOW!" said the owl,
as the pretty red butterflies
flew by.

She watched them land on the bright **orange** flowers, which opened up in the warm sunshine.

Up in the sky the clouds turned
grey and it started to rain.

But the sun was still shining.

"WOW!" said the owl, as a beautiful rainbow filled the sky with colour.

The little owl sat
happily in her tree,
and watched as the
sun went down . . .

. . . and the moon came up.

The daytime is full of beautiful
colours, she thought.

But, "WOW!" said the owl.
"The night-time stars are the
most beautiful of all."

Too excited to sleep, the little owl stayed awake ALL night long, just like little owls are supposed to do.

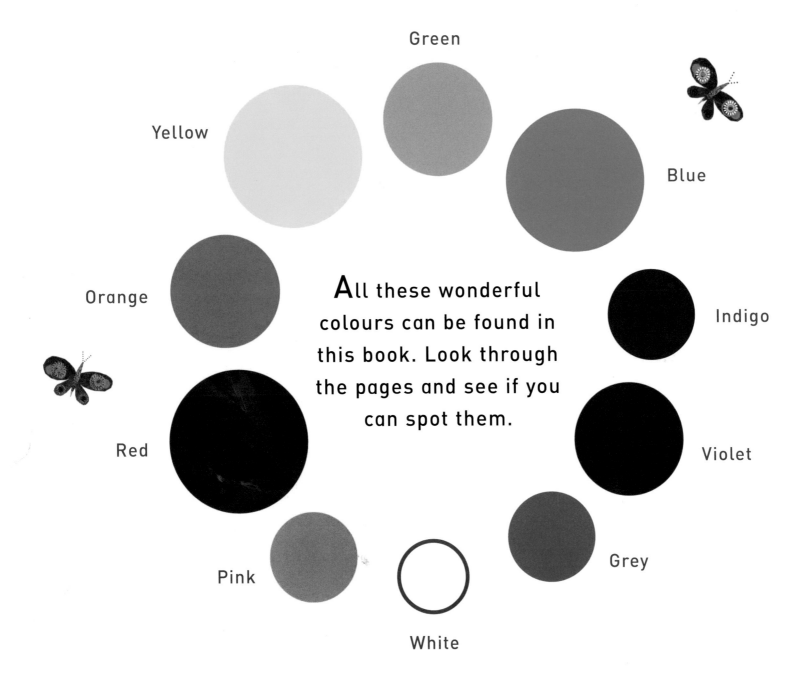

Green

Yellow

Blue

Orange

Indigo

All these wonderful colours can be found in this book. Look through the pages and see if you can spot them.

Red

Violet

Pink

Grey

White